Departed Souls

Shadows that follow you

By

Sneha Alekh Shah

Published by: The Writer's Cosmos
ISBN: 978-81-971356-4-4

Title: Departed Souls
Author: Sneha Alekh Shah

Cover Design: Gayatri Sengar
Printed in: Mumbai
For permission requests, contact the publisher at:
mail@thewriterscosmos.com

ACKNOWLEDGEMENTS

I want to express my deepest gratitude to all those who have supported me throughout this journey of writing and publishing this book.

I am immensely thankful to my family for their unwavering love, encouragement, and understanding during the ups and downs of the creative process. Their belief in me kept me going, even when doubts crept in.

A special thanks to Miss. Gayatri Sengar and the entire team of THE WRITER'S COSMOS, for their consistent support and respect for my work through my creative journey. Your expertise and guidance were invaluable and greatly appreciated.

Lastly, I express my heartfelt appreciation to the readers who will embark on this literary journey with me. Your interest and support mean the world to me.

Thank you, from the bottom of my heart.

Sneha Alekh Shah

ABOUT THE BOOK

"Departed Souls: The Shadows that Follow You" delves into the depths of the human psyche, weaving a gripping tale of mystery, psychological turmoil, and self-discovery. As protagonist Rahul embarks on a journey to the serene hills, he stumbles upon an enigmatic woman whose presence triggers a cascade of unsettling memories from his past.

Haunted by the shadows of his childhood, Rahul finds himself entangled in a web of secrets and unresolved traumas. As he grapples with his inner demons, the line between past and present blurs, plunging him into a gripping psychological thriller where reality and illusion intertwine.

With each turn of the page, readers are drawn deeper into Rahul's descent into darkness, questioning what is real and what is merely a figment of his tortured mind. Yet, amidst the chaos, glimmers of hope emerge as Rahul embarks on a journey of self-discovery, confronting his past to find redemption in the present.

"Departed Souls: The Shadows that Follow You" is a riveting exploration of the human psyche, a haunting tale that will leave readers on the edge of their seats until the very last page. Prepare to be enthralled, captivated, and ultimately, transformed by this unforgettable psychological thriller.

Contents....

Chapter 1: 'Heights' of vulnerability

Present Day, Manali

Rahul was bored at the resort. He picked up his backpack and moved out to take a stroll at the nearby hill. He was looking for a place from where he could enjoy the beautiful sunset when his eyes caught a visual that terrified him.

"Hey!! Miss!!! What do you think you're doing?" Rahul nearly shouted at a stranger girl standing on a high cliff.

"I'm trying to die! Get out of here." She said sternly without turning her back! Rahul ran towards her, pulled her hand, and brought her back down.

His eyes were stuck at the vulnerable face of Navya, whose dry, red eyes were speaking volumes about her mental condition. He was petrified by her determination to end her life!

"Do you even know how many people crave for the life you are living?" Rahul tried to make her understand.

"Oh! Please! Don't even begin lecturing me about the importance of being able to live! I've seen it all." Said Navya bluntly.

"Have you? Really?" Rahul asked peeping down her eyes.

Navya tried to break the eye contact. She was about to move back to the highest point of the cliff when Rahul dragged her down again.

"Listen, miss! I don't know who you are or what has happened with you, and believe me, I'm least interested to know! But, I'm not letting you do this in front of my eyes. So you better tell me where your group is. I'm going to drop you off with them." Said Rahul.

"I'm alone. No one from my family knows where I am." Navya said rudely.

"Where have you come from?" Asked Rahul.

"Why do you think I'd tell you that? Mister, just get out of my way. You have no idea what I have been through. Just let me go. You go, live your life. Let me end mine!!" Navya nearly ordered the stranger standing in front of her.

Rahul said nothing. He held her hand and started walking towards the resort he was staying in. Navya tried to escape but in vain. Rahul took her to the resort garden and made her sit on a bench. He offered her some water and let her relax.

"First of all, tell me your name!"

"Navya Sethi."

"Okay Navya! I'm Rahul and here's the deal. I'm not letting you die, get that straight. I'm here for a few more days. Why don't you join me for the rest of your trip? I might help you change your mind about dying." Rahul tried convincing her.

Navya mindlessly agreed. Rahul dialled a number.

"Hey, where are you? Come down to the garden." He said on the phone.
In a few minutes, Shreya arrived at the spot. Rahul saw that she looked surprised to see him with a girl

who was seemingly distressed. Her questioning eyes made him narrate the entire story to Shreya, his girlfriend.

"So what are we planning to do with her?" Shreya asked Rahul taking him to a corner.

"I've no idea. She is unwilling to give any details about her family. I don't know what to do next." Rahul stated keeping a constant eye on Navya. "Shreya, I hope you're fine with this. I know it's unlikely for me to do something like this but this is what I have to do." Rahul said with fear in his voice.

"Of course, Rahul. I understand. It's very kind of you to do this. I'm proud of you." Shreya hugged him with pride.

They returned to where Navya was seated. She accompanied them to a bonfire party happening nearby. Everyone was enjoying the live music and food when Rahul found Navya missing. He instantly panicked. He looked around for her when he saw a shadow of her sitting on a nearby hill. He ran to rescue her, again.

"What are you doing here?" Rahul asked her calmly.

"Waiting for you to find me." Navya replied staring into nothingness. "Come, join me." She gestured him.

He silently walked towards her and sat next to her. She placed her palm on his hand looking into his eyes. He thoughtfully assured her that she wasn't alone.

"We're here for you Navya. I don't know what has led you here but there's something called destiny, you know. It can't merely be a coincidence that I found you there this evening." Rahul said, trying to make sense out of the situation.

"It definitely wasn't! It was meant to be. You were meant to save me from dying AGAIN." She looked at him with a smile so strange that he had never seen before.

"Rahul!!! What are you doing up there?" Shreya called out to him. He looked down and gestured her that he'd be right there. He turned back to hold Navya's hand and take her back but she was not there anymore!!! SHE HAD VANISHED!!
Did she jump off the cliff?

Chapter 2: Engulfed by the guilt

Rahul was devastated with the fact that she was nowhere to be seen. The cliff was high and cold. It was terribly dark. He had no information about Navya apart from her name. He was helpless. His nerves went cold, his eyes went dry. He was motionless. Shreya somehow managed to take him to their room.

Rahul went to sleep without a word being spoken. Shreya too was exhausted to ask him anything. She dozed off as well.

The night seemed to be the longest to them. Ultimately, the sun shone and they were awake. Rahul was still in a different zone. Shreya was feeling better. She stood headstrong with him.

They returned to Mumbai, their hometown. Their routine life had started. Rahul and Shreya had rented a lavish apartment in Mumbai and were a live in couple for half a decade now. They both worked at the same MNC as IT professionals. They had a stable life. They were planning on getting married soon. They were practically married, just the formalities

were left!
"Rahul, you need to let it go." Rahul heard Shreya tell him as he was staring blankly at the ceiling lying in his bed.

"How? How can I let it go, Shreya? It's been two weeks since we have returned and all I can do is think about that girl. It was in my control to save a life and I couldn't." Rahul said with a tone coated with guilt.

"Exactly! It's been fifteen days!! You need to come out of it. It was her destiny to die." Shreya tried to explain.

Destiny!! The word caught his attention. His mind started going back to the night when Navya jumped off the cliff. "She had said something about destiny!" Rahul thought to himself.

Seeing Rahul lost in thoughts again, Shreya went to sleep in frustration.

Rahul's mind was storming with a number of questions. His conscience was propelling him to find out who Navya was and what led her to take such a drastic step! He immediately turned on his iPad. He opened Shreya's Facebook profile as he had none on social media! He typed in her name 'Navya Sethi'. A number of profiles appeared on screen. He restlessly scrolled down the page. His fingers stopped at one of the pictures of Navya. His eyes lit up with relief. They welled up seeing her bright smile in the picture. His eyes cried rivers after two weeks of sheer dryness in them. He clicked on the profile with shivering fingers. His heart was beating faster than ever with anxiety. Navya's profile appeared in front of his eyes. He opened her picture and stared at her vibrant face for what it seemed like an eternity. He heartily apologised to her for not being able to save her life. His tears needed no words to express how guilty and helpless he felt.

After the resentment, he started looking through her profile. He came to know of her school, her friends, family. He came to know that she had been married. He saw her husband's profile as well. He saw their happy pictures too. His mind again went on to a thinking spree. "What made her kill herself? She seemed to be a happy person. A nice family, a happy marriage. What might have happened that she did this? What about her family? What about her husband? Did she have kids?" A series of questions surrounded his mind. He scrolled down more to see a post by her husband. He had written a long note. Rahul read out the note:

"Dear Navya, we promised a forever together. Where are you now? You broke the pact, you cheater!!! What would I do without you? We were expecting our first child. You took it away with you. I'm left with nothing but your memories. They haunt me now. I wish you'd take me with you too. Come back, now! Or take me along! The moments we spent together are all I have and that's unfair!!!

Thank you for everything. Be happy wherever you are. I love you, always.

Yours,
Avinash."

Rahul was crushed and heartbroken. He cursed himself for not stopping her from jumping off the cliff that night. He thought he killed a family. His eyes were red with excruciating pain and guilt. He gathered himself and was about to shut off the iPad when the date of the post caught his attention! The post was dated March 3rd, 2018!!

Navya had been dead for FIVE YEARS???!!!! HOW!???

Chapter 3: What just happened?

"What? She's been dead for five years? Then how come I met her just a few days back? Or she never died?" Rahul dozed off to sleep with a million questions running on his mind.

It was a new morning. Rahul woke up to see Shreya had left for office. He was two hours late for work. He unlocked his phone to check if Shreya had left any message for him. "Rahul, I don't know what is wrong with you. Ever since we have returned from Manali, you've been acting weird. I think you should take a break from work. Think over it." Her message read.

Rahul knew she was right. He had to think over things. He was still not sure if what he came across the previous night was true or just a nightmare. The girl who he met a few days back was dead since years? His brain was split into numerous pieces he could not gather in place!

He thought of something and started packing his bags! He then left the house in a frenzy. He dropped a message to Shreya: "I know you're right. I need some time off. I'm going out of town for a few days. I will stay in touch. Take care."

His questions needed answers. His life was upside down after the previous night. He could not think straight. He did not know where his life was leading him to. He knew something was off. He knew he could do something to make everything right.

He took the next train to Manali. He booked the same resort to stay in. It was about 10 pm when he reached the resort. He placed his luggage in the room and went out to the garden to take a stroll, rather to statistically analyse the series of events. Just when he was about to go back to his room after a couple of hours, he spotted a girl near the cliff. He knew it was her. He was terrified at the mere thought.

"Navya?" He called out with sheer fear.

"I pulled you back here, didn't I?" She said with a smile still with her back towards him.

"What are you doing, Navya? I'm going crazy thinking about you." Rahul said running towards her.

"That crazy, huh? I like that." Her tone was dipped in naughtiness.

"This is no time to do this! What's your mystery? How come I saw your death post on your Facebook profile? Were you never dead and you're fooling your family? Where's your child? He must be a five year old now, right?" Rahul threw a bucket of questions at her.

"Which world are you living in, Rahul? Facebook? Really? You think people write true stories there?" Navya said sarcastically.

"So you know! You know there's a post there about your death! What is it?" Rahul asked.

"Rahul, you've just come here. You've anyway applied for a long leave at your high profile 'IT' job, haven't you? We have a lot of time together. Go to your room and have a good sleep!" Navya said with a strange smile.

"No wait!! You can't do this! I need answers!" Rahul nearly yelled.

Just then, his attention was caught by the flickering light behind him. He turned around to see what was wrong. He saw that the light was just fine. When he turned back, she was gone!! Vanished!! AGAIN!!! He was frustrated. He entered the resort and moved towards the reception. He asked the receptionist if there was a guest named Navya Sethi living in the resort. The receptionist denied. Rahul was dangerously stuck in a loop. He could not find any link to this mystery woman. He did just what Navya had asked him to do. He went to his room and tried to rest.

Rahul was in deep sleep when his eyes started flickering with flashes of his encounters with Navya! Her enchanting smile, her distressed form, her undone hair, the scars on her arms and neck, her drained out voice! Everything was flashing in front of his eyes when they suddenly shut open and he sat upright on his bed.

"How did she know I work as an IT professional? She doesn't know anything about me apart from my first name! I don't even have any social media profiles! How is this even possible? Has she been stalking me? Is she doing all this purposefully? If yes, what is her purpose?" His mind questioned!!

Chapter 4: Digging the past

It was 4 in the morning when Rahul found himself drenched in sweat with all the nightmares. He was petrified yet he wanted to dig deeper into Navya's history. He was curious to know why his mind was so involved in her story that he did not care about anything else but her. Strangled in these thoughts, he moved out of his room to the cliff he saw Navya the previous night. She was there again, sitting on the cliff facing her back at him.

"Good morning, mister!" She said to Rahul without turning back.

"What are you doing here, Navya? You have a wonderful family, I saw it. Why aren't you with them? Why don't you tell them you're alive?" Rahul bombarded her with these questions.

"Do you think they'd care if I were alive?" Her tone had a severe pain.

"Why won't they? Your husband seems to be lost. He loves you, he was broken when he thought you were dead. Anyway, how did you die? I mean what made the world think you were dead?" Rahul seemed to be bewildered in himself.

"Is this your first trip to Manali?" Navya asked out of the blue.

"I've been here before. This resort is one of our favourites here. Shreya and I usually celebrate our special days by visiting this wonderful city." Rahul said with a cheerful smile.

"Shreya? Your wife?" Navya asked.

"Almost a wife! (Laughs) We're getting married soon. The last time we were here, I was going to propose to her but then you happened!!! You ruined my plans. I had to leave her alone at home to see you again." Said Rahul in agitation.

Navya laughed softly at his words.

"When did you visit Manali earlier than the last time?" Navya's question irritated Rahul now.

"Why does she need to know that?" He thought to himself.

"We celebrated our 1st anniversary as a couple here in 2018. It was an amazing experience." He managed to answer her without getting mad.

"What did you experience then?" Navya asked.

"I realised how madly I was in love with Shreya. I realised that she was the one I would want to spend the rest of my life with. We were high on love and drinks too! I vaguely remember a night when we were madly drunk. When she dozed off, she looked like an angel to me. I covered her in the warmth of the blanket. I needed some fresh air. I went out of the resort to take a stroll." Rahul was immersed in telling his story. His expressions changed, he seemed to be trying to remember something.

"I have a blurry image of an incident. It was dark, just some dim lights coming from the resort. I was walking when I heard a broken scream of a woman. She was saying, 'Don't do this, please. I'm pregnant. I have a life in me, please don't take two lives.' She was sobbing profusely. I remember walking in the direction of the voice. I saw a woman standing at the edge of the cliff whose one hand was on her abdomen trying to hold her baby, other was held by a man in front of her covered in a long black coat with a hood." Rahul said with his eyes closed as he was recreating the vision in his head.

"Do you remember her face?" Navya asked softly.

Rahul's chain of thoughts broke on hearing her soft voice. He opened his eyes and there was the face he was trying to recall. He jumped up on his place and fearfully ran down the cliff.

"It was you! I saw you that night. You were screaming to be saved. Someone was trying to push you down the cliff." Rahul cried in terror.

"Yes, it was me. Do you remember me pleading the man not to kill me?" Navya confessed.

"Yes, yes I remember. You were calling out his name too. You were calling him 'Dev'. Who is Dev? Who tried to kill you, Navya? What happened after that? Why can't I remember? Did he push you? Or you were able to escape? What happened???" Rahul's tears were uncontrollable. His eyes went red and his heart rate went dangerously high. He was going breathless.

"I now remember I didn't want to be involved in such a situation. I was drunk and exhausted. I stepped back from there and was about to run to the resort when I heard the man saying, 'I'm sorry Navya. Oh no, I'm sorry Mrs. Navya Avinash Sethi!' He was laughing. I was terrified. I ran back to my room. This is all I remember." Rahul was directionless. He didn't know what he was going through.

"Avinash Sethi." Navya's eyes welled up at the name.

"Rahul, please be with him. He must be lonely. He must need someone." Navya said with grief.

"Me? How would that help him? I don't even know him. Why don't you contact him? Why can't you? It's been five years, Navya." Rahul tried to explain her.

"What if he has moved on? What if he is happy now? I just need to know if he is fine." Navya seemed clueless about what she was saying.

"Okay, I saw on his Facebook , he's in Delhi. I'll go to Delhi to see him, to find out how he's doing." Rahul consoled her.

"Thank you, Rahul. You go. I'm safe here." Navya placed her palm on his, assuring him of her safety.

Rahul started walking towards the resort, he turned around once to look at her. This time, she was there, smiling at him with tears in her eyes. He gave her a consoling smile and turned back to the resort.

"Hey babe! I'm safe, don't you worry. I'll be home once I get to the roots of something that's bothering me. Remember, I love you." Rahul's message to Shreya read.

He checked out of the resort and took the next bus to

Delhi! Delhi! Avinash Sethi! Will Rahul reach Delhi? If he does, will he be able to find Avinash? Who is Dev? Why did he try to kill Navya?

Chapter 5: The Demons of the past!

"Rahul! What are you doing here? Go to your room and sleep!" Rahul heard his mother scolding him for peeping in his parents' room in the middle of the night. Rahul saw his father with a belt in his hand and his mother sitting at the edge of the bed holding her saree pallu against her cheek as if to hide something. He closed the door but could hear his mother's painful screams after a whisk of the belt.

Rahul was shaken by these visuals in his dream again. He could never know what used to happen behind that closed door. He was hardly eight when his mother died of cardiac arrest. His father too passed away soon after. He was raised by his maternal aunt in Mumbai. His memory always had this blurry image of his parents behind the closed door.

His eyes opened due to sharp brakes. He saw that his bus had reached Delhi. He de-boarded the bus and took a taxi to his hotel. When Rahul searched, he realised that Avinash Sethi was a big name in the construction world in Delhi. He was a renowned builder. It wasn't a difficult task to find where the most successful builder of the city lived. As Rahul reached the Sethi Residence, he saw a party going on in the main garden of the grand villa. He entered as a guest. A little girl of about three came running out of the villa and jumped up on a man who seemed to be her farther. The man turned around and Rahul was surprised to see Avinash with his daughter. He saw the little girl cut her birthday cake holding her parents' hands. Everything was cheerful around. He realised that Navya was utterly right. Avinash has moved on. He is happy now. He has a family, a happy family.

"Should I tell him about Navya? What if it hinders his happiness? But it is his right to know that she's alive." Rahul was in a dilemma. He softly moved out of the party and went back to his hotel.

Rahul was not sure what to do next. His fingers unintentionally dialled Shreya's number. She picked up immediately and Rahul lost all his senses on hearing the voice he had been craving for for so long.

"Rahul, what happened? Where are you? You do know I'm always with you, right? Tell me what's wrong. I might just help." Shreya said in the softest tone possible.

"I'm in Delhi. I'm here to do something I'm not sure if

I should do or not. Help me, Shreya. It's haunting me now. I feel I'm stuck in a loop of endless questions. What do I do?" Rahul broke down.

"Come home." Shreya stated.

"I can't. I have committed to someone. You know me, I don't keep loose ends. I'll come home once I know I've done the right thing. Till then, be with me." He said and disconnected the call.

Rahul then worked on a plan of action. He decided to befriend Avinash before telling him anything about Navya. The next day, he went to Avinash's office- 'Navya Construction' as a buyer. They talked about business for sometime. Rahul found a gap to talk about something personal to Avinash.

"So, Navya Construction! Nice name. Anyone from the family?" Rahul asked.

"Yeah, my first wife." Avinash's facial expressions changed.

Rahul stayed quiet.

"She passed away in an accident about five years ago. I was devastated after her. But then, life must go on. So I married my current wife Amrita and we have a beautiful daughter. We named her Navya. I'm grateful that Amrita let me name her that." Avinash said with a painful smile.

Rahul didn't know what to say. His senses were frozen. He left after a formal goodbye. He took the next flight out to Mumbai. He reached home and rang the doorbell. Shreya came to open the door and broke down in tears on seeing him. They went in and had dinner together after what felt like an eternity to them.

"We are going to Delhi," Rahul stated out of the blue.

"Delhi? Why?" Shreya asked, perplexed.

Rahul gave her each and every detail of his experience. He didn't know if Shreya would understand but he had to let it out.

"Avinash must know about her being alive." Shreya said just what Rahul wanted to hear.

"I know! I have a plan. Just play along. Please." Rahul requested. She nodded supportively.

Rahul had something in mind. But what? Will it work? Will Avinash ever know of Navya being alive?

Chapter 6: The Plan of Action

Rahul and Shreya took the next flight to Delhi. As soon as they reached, Rahul called up Navya Constructions for an appointment with Avinash. After days of formal meetings, Avinash invited them to his place for dinner- just what Rahul was looking for. Shreya easily befriended Amrita and baby Navya. They all had dinner together.

"Let's go to Manali next week." Rahul said intriguingly.

Avinash's face turned pale. "Manali? Why Manali?" His voice had a noticeable quiver. His eyes shifted on Amrita who had a strange fear on her face. Avinash looked back at Rahul waiting for the answer to his question.

"It's our place! We always celebrate our special occasions there. We just love that place. Let us all go there together. It'll be a memorable trip, I'm sure!" Rahul said with glee in his voice. After a lot of hesitation from Avinash and Amrita, Rahul and Shreya could finally convince them for the trip. Shreya invited a friend of hers, Karan and his wife Ruhi as well to the trip so as to make sure that

Avinash doesn't develop any doubts regarding the trip.

"Manali? Avinash, we can't go there! Why don't you understand?" Amrita said to Avinash once they were in their bedroom after everyone had left.

"It's been five years, Amrita. Just let go of that incident. We are doing well. I'll be fine, I promise." Avinash tried to calm her. He managed to convince her with great deal of love and affection.

All the three couples left for Manali the next week. Rahul booked the same resort they always stayed in. "What next?" Asked Shreya. "Let's wait for the right time. I need to know where Navya is currently. I'm going out to look for her." Rahul said.

"I'll be with Karan and Ruhi for a while. They should not feel left out." Shreya said.

"Yes, please."

As Rahul moved out of the room, he waited for Navya at the cliff. He could not keep in touch with her during his visit to Delhi as she had said she didn't keep any phone with her. She had told him that he'd find her at the same place where he had left her before.

"So, you are back?" Rahul heard Navya's voice. He turned around to see Navya with overwhelmed eyes.

"Avinash is married now. He has a lovely family. Yet, I thought he should know about you being alive. I have brought him and his family here. I'll make him meet you whenever you say." Rahul said in one breath.

"He is married to his secretary, Amrita, right? Anyway, bring him here tomorrow morning, alone, just him and you!!" Navya said and went away.

Rahul was confused. How did she know that he married Amrita after the apparent death of Navya? He found it really strange. "But everything I am experiencing for a month now is strange!!!" He thought to himself!!

"Meet me at the cliff tomorrow at 5 am." Rahul's message to Avinash read.

Next morning, Rahul sat at the cliff waiting for Avinash.

"Navya, I am here. Avinash will be here soon." Rahul said staring into nothingness.

It is about to happen. Navya and Avinash face to face! What will happen now?

Chapter 7: Facing your fears

Rahul waited for Avinash and Navya in great anticipation. Hours passed but there was no sign of any of them. Rahul started panicking, what if something wrong had happened to her! His mind wondered recklessly. He tried calling Avinash. His phone was switched off. Rahul didn't know what to do as he felt Navya had betrayed him. His effort for her seemed to fail as she was now vanished. He was restless, not knowing what to do next, he claimed up the cliff and shouted Navya's name at the top of his voice! No response still!!! He cried profusely to the unexpected turn of events! He kept shouting her name in panic when his foot slipped on the top of the high cliff!! Before he could fathom the incident, he was pulled down the cliff by Karan, Shreys's friend. When Rahul gained his senses, he saw Karan, Ruhi and Shreya standing right there in front of him.

"What happened, Rahul? Where's Navya? Did they meet?? What is going on?" Shreya asked.

"I don't know Shreya! Navya never arrived here nor did Avinash. I waited for her for hours! But there's no sign of her. I have no idea why she did that to me.

I'm afraid if she is safe or not!! Why didn't she come????" Said Rahul completely frustrated.

"Because she's really dead." Karan stated blankly. His statement stunned Rahul.

"How? When? I met her last night! How is this even possible?" Rahul questioned.

"Let's go to the resort, Rahul. Let's talk there." Shreya held his hand and took him to their room. All four of them sat down. Rahul gulped down a glass of water as soon as he could.

"Rahul, Shreya had discussed your experiences with me since you got back to Mumbai the very first time after you encountered Navya. Now listen to me very carefully." Karan spoke as he saw Rahul getting back normal.

There was subtle silence in the room. Shreya had not left Rahul's hand even for a moment. She knew he needed her. He needed her to understand what was coming his way now. She signalled Karan to continue.

"Listen, my friend! I know everything you've been experiencing for such a long time. Let Shreya tell you what exactly is going on!" Karan stated.

"When you came to the resort with Navya for the very first time, I could not see her. Only you knew she was with us. I was scared initially but slowly I realised this was deep-rooted. So I decided to go along with you on whatever you were asking me to do or what you wanted to do. When you came here after Navya leaving me in Mumbai, I knew something was extremely serious. I searched Navya's profile on social media and got to know that she was dead long ago. I somehow managed to track her parents' number and called them up. What they told me shocked me to the core." Shreya spoke as her hand caressed the back of Rahul's palm constantly.

Rahul seemed to be completely lost. His brain wasn't really accepting whatever he was hearing.

"Her parents told me that Navya had died 5 years back. Her body was recovered from the valley under the cliff and her last rites were performed by her family immediately after." Shreya continued.

"What? How is that even possible? I met her, Shreya!!! I HAVE MET HER!! Why don't you people understand?" Rahul seemed to be defensive.

"You only imagined meeting her." Ruhi said out of the blue.

"Imagined? What the hell is wrong with all of you? I don't even know you people and you are judging me on my experiences? How in the world do you know that I have been only imagining a girl whose existence has been proven by herself, her family!" Rahul was still in disbelief and now agitated with Karan and Ruhi, complete strangers to him!

What is going on? Is Navya really dead? Then who did Rahul meet? Was he really imagining her???

Chapter 8: The past and the present!

11 years ago, Rahul & Shreys's college campus

"Shreya! You can't run away from me!!" Kunal held Shreya's hand firmly wanting to hurt her.

"You're hurting me, Kunal! Just leave my hand and let me go!!!!" Shreya screamed in pain.

"I won't. I love you. Stay with me or you know what I can do!" Kunal tried to intimidate her.

"I do know what you are. And believe me Kunal, I'm not going to shut up!"

"This will shut you up right away!" Said Kunal raising his hand to slap her just when she withdrew herself from him, "Don't you dare Kunal" Shreya's eyes were filled with rage and disgust. Rage for herself that she ever let a man like Kunal be with her and disgust for a man who thinks that abusing his beloved is the new love language! She ran away from him.

Rahul was a distant spectator to all this. His one-sided feelings for Shreya increased manifold. Slowly, he approached her and eventually they fell in love. Rahul once narrated this story to Shreya and told her that he had seen it from a distance.

"No man has a right to hit a woman. Hitting or abusing his partner doesn't make him a man." Rahul had said to Shreya with his vision lost in some wonderment. Upon Shreya's asking, Rahul had told her about this dream of his that kept chasing him since he lost his mother to a cardiac arrest.

Shreya started to realise that Rahul had been struggling with his past as his parents had never shared a good bond. All he knew about them was that his father ill-treated his mother. He was too young to understand the gravity of something this horrible. He was naive. He didn't realise his mother needed him, his support, his love. But his young age couldn't help her and she eventually died of a cardiac arrest. His father also passed away soon after to some disease he was not even interested to know about.

Present day, Manali

"When you narrated me everything what had happened with you in Manali, I started to realise it had to do something with your past. I called up Karan, who by the way is a psychologist. We met when you had gone back to Manali and I told him everything. He too supported my instinct that you feeling Navya's presence surely had a connection to your mother's passing. We analysed everything. Then, one day I got your personal diary. I read about the dreams you kept having about your parents. As we investigated deeper, our doubts turned to reality. Navya was really dead and you had just been getting hallucinations about her." Shreya tried to calm down an anxious Rahul.

"Your subconscious mind was trying to help a girl who died years ago simply because you couldn't do the same for your mother. Your blurry image of her falling off the cliff generated an imaginary story around her death and convinced you that it was a murder while it was simply an accident."

"So, you know about that? You know I had seen Navya before she really died?" Rahul asked Shreya.

"Yes, it's all there in your diary. I'm so sorry I went through your personal stuff but believe me that was the only way to save you from this emotional trauma." Shreya apologized.

Rahul was still devastated.

"But, if she was just my imagination, how do I know so much about her? Her name, her being pregnant? About Avinash?? How??" Rahul was still in disbelief.

"You must have heard something from Navya, her name, Avinash's name, before she actually fell off the cliff. You have simply built up a story around it. Everything else is something your brain has developed. She wasn't murdered. She fell off the cliff by accident, her parents have confirmed that." Karan tried to explain.

"Why couldn't I see her this morning? If it was all my imagination, why couldn't I imagine her then?" Asked Rahul.

"Because you never knew how your parents interacted with each other. Whatever you have known about them was all behind the door. Your brain couldn't imagine a conversation between Navya and Avinash." Karan stated. "Your brain only imagines things you already know."

"If you all knew this, why did you let me bring Avinash here?" Rahul asked.

"Because we wanted you to realise everything on your own. If we had denied you to come here, you could not be convinced of all this." Shreya said. "Also, I had deleted your message to Avinash last night. I didn't want him to know what was going on. That's the reason he didn't come to the cliff."

Rahul realised what they wanted to say. Yet, there was something that was bothering him. He partly accepted the fact that he had been hallucinating about Navya. His mind accepted the truth but his heart! His heart still went out to Navya. Her pain, her unborn child, her death. How could this be the end of her story? How can she just be a fragment of his imagination? How???

Not getting any answers, Rahul agreed to return

home. He promised Shreya that he'll start taking a treatment for his mental wellness. Shreya managed to convince Rahul not to tell anything to Avinash and his family. They were happy after years of pain and grief. Rahul agreed mindlessly.

Chapter 9: THE END!??

All the three couples enjoyed their trip to the beautiful hill station. Rahul's mind was now off Navya. He shut his thoughts down. He was with Shreya, and that's all mattered to him. His love for Shreya had grown limitlessly, after what all she had done for him. He thought it was his turn to give her everything she deserved.
Next morning, they had a flight back to Mumbai from Delhi. They all rented a cab to Delhi airport where they'd be saying a final goodbye to Avinash, Amrita and little Navya! It was about time. Avinash and Amrita collected their luggage, greeted the others and started walking towards their car.

"Rahul!" Rahul heard Navya's whispering voice, again, at DELHI airport! He shut his ears with his palms and closed his eyes! He was trying to silence the imaginary voices in his head. When he opened his eyes, he saw Navya standing in front of him, "Stop Dev!" She said.

"Dev??" Rahul thought to himself. "That's the man who killed Navya! But that was just my hallucination! Dev is a fictional name my head made up!" Rahul was mingled in these thoughts.

"Stop him, now! Just stop him!!!" Rahul heard Navya screaming.

"Dev!! Stop!" Rahul shouted.

"Hey!! How do you know that name? That's what my college gang used to call me!!" Avinash said turning around!!

The END…….or the beginning of something??

www.ingramcontent.com/pod-product-compliance
Lightning Source LLC
Chambersburg PA
CBHW062203160726
48282CB00027B/982
* 9 7 8 8 1 9 7 1 3 5 6 4 4 *